WOMAN on TOP

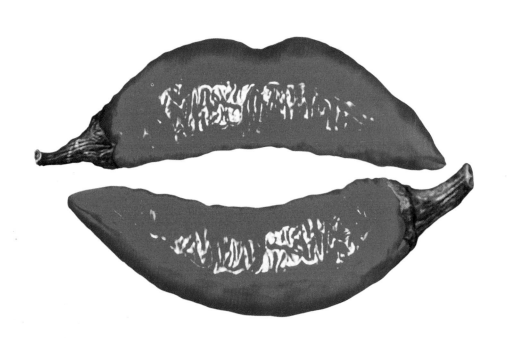

WOMAN ON TOP

a sexy, delicious fairy tale

BASED ON THE MOTION PICTURE WRITTEN BY VERA BLASI

VERA BLASI and FINA TORRES

illustrated by JUSTINE GASQUET

ReganBooks
An Imprint of HarperCollinsPublishers

HarperCollins books may be purchased for educational, business, or sales promotional use. For information please write: Special Markets Department, HarperCollins Publishers Inc., 10 East 53rd Street, New York, NY 10022.

Illustrations © 2000 by Justine Gasquet

Designed by Charles Rue Woods

First Edition

Printed on acid-free paper

Library of Congress Cataloging-in-Publication Data has been applied for.

ISBN 0-06-039396-3

00 01 02 03 04 RRD 10 9 8 7 6 5 4 3 2 1

To Yemanjá, Queen of the Yoruba, goddess of the sea, of the fish, of the life and death of the fisherman, virgin of the sailors, temptress of our hearts, priestess of the subtle world, keeper of the salt, siren of the tides, nymph of the currents, enchantress of the harbor, daughter of the waves, sorceress of the whirlpools, maiden of the foam and spray, link between the solid and the liquid, our lady of the perpetual blue, saint of the silver moon, princess of the white roses, mermaid of our tears, mirror of our reflection, interpreter of our dreams, angel of the silent world, sleeping beauty of the ocean floor, lifter of the veil, the deep feminine mystery, hostess of the all-knowing unconscious, owner of the truth, guardian of our secrets, mother of all the Orishás, the beginning, the middle, and the end. Odoiá!

"What's worse than not getting what you want?"

"Getting what you want."

Once upon a time, in a faraway land known

as Brazil, there lived a girl named Isabella.

When she was born, the gods blessed her with extraordinary beauty, but overlooked one itty-bitty flaw...

motion sickness. She got carsick, stroller-sick, even elevator-sick! But this was Bahia, a region of Brazil where the palm trees seemed to bend toward Africa, home of the Yoruba gods. Brought to the New World in the bowels of slave ships, they now reigned on both continents. These deities, or *orishás*, were tremendously powerful, but none of them more respected than Yemanjá, goddess of the sea.

Witnessing the suffering of the motion-sick child,
mistake and compensated her with a gift…

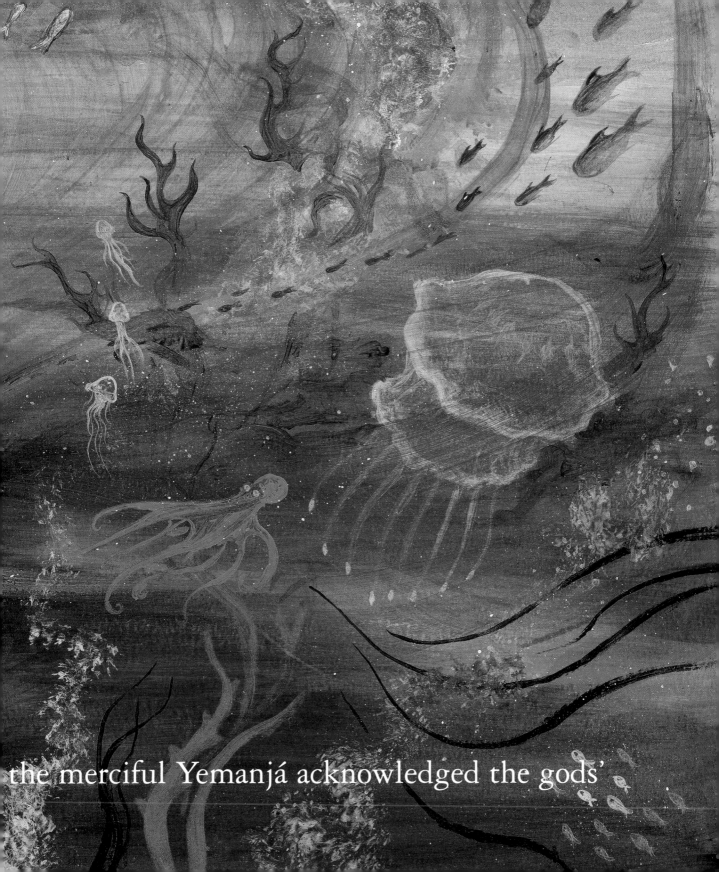

the merciful Yemanjá acknowledged the gods'

And so little Isabella spent her days in the kitchen with Olivia, the family cook. There, amid the smells of simmering spices and bubbling concoctions, she discovered the goddess's precious gift to her: a magic touch for cooking. Isabella blossomed into a dazzling young woman, with long hair and a radiant smile, who could melt the palates and hearts of men. A pinch of salt, a handful of peppers, a drop of coconut milk—Isabella had the Midas touch for spicing, turning all her dishes into gold. She dreamed of some day going abroad and becoming a famous chef.

But one man was about to sweep away Isabella's dreams: the handsome and dashing Toninho. Bronzed from the sun and with stars in his eyes, he was looking for a new chef for his restaurant when he stumbled upon the beautiful Isabella. When they laid eyes upon each other, they knew instantly that they were meant to be together forever. It was love at first bite!

So they married, certain they would live happily ever after. Whenever they embraced, they understood how oil felt when it bubbled against the bottom of a hot skillet. Whenever they kissed, they knew how a chili pepper felt when it was crushed and the heat from its insides was released. And when they made love, they knew how the crushed pepper felt when it fell into the skillet's sizzling oil.

So great was their love that everything around them seemed to be imbued with the same kind of magic. The tropical sun shone even brighter, and the South Atlantic Ocean brimmed with fish. Isabella's exotic dishes turned Toninho's restaurant into one of the most popular spots in Bahia. People came from all over the country just to taste her exquisite cuisine.

But hidden in the kitchen, she did all the work;
singing to the customers, he got all the credit.

And though she knew that her talents could get her jobs in the best restaurants in the world, Isabella's dreams of international glory would melt away in Toninho's irresistible embrace…

Alas, even the most passionate of lovers have to learn to compromise some-times. Isabella could live with her husband's need for attention as long as he could live with her little affliction. She still suffered from motion sickness, which she could manage only by controlling her motions. As long as she always drove the car, always led when they danced, always stayed on top when they made love, everything was fine—for her, that is, but not for Toninho. As time went by, his male pride got the better of his good judgment. Increasingly obsessed with this position problem, Toninho made an *un*manly decision, one that he would seriously regret.... He decided he had to have a missionary-position intermission.

"I'm a man! I have to be on top sometimes!" he claimed when Isabella caught him…on top…of an accommodating lass.

Inconsolable, Isabella wept oceans of tears as she prayed to the goddess, who always looked after her. "Give me the strength, Yemanjá. Please, give me the strength to leave him—and Bahia." The goddess answered her plea with a clap of thunder and a bolt of lightning! So Isabella impulsively packed her belongings and fled to San Francisco—airsick all the way—to live with Monica, her best friend since childhood.

The night she left, Toninho walked every inch of the city, looking for his wife. She was nowhere to be found. Anguished, he went to the beach where the locals were honoring Yemanjá in a breathtaking ceremony. Thunderous, percussive music accompanied the procession, led by the *Baianas,* famous for the captivating way they dressed: brilliant white lace dresses that ballooned around them like parachutes, white turbans, and tons of colorful beaded necklaces. They headed toward the shallows, balancing large trays of food and flowers on their heads—offerings to the sea goddess. The fishermen followed the *Baianas,* giving thanks to the mermaid queen for the bountiful fish she provided.

Toninho pushed his way through the procession and caught up to Serafina, the dreaded, cigar-smoking, high priestess witch doctor. He demanded to be told where his wife had gone, but Serafina only scolded him: *"Malandro, safado, sem-vergonha*—you naughty, shameless scoundrel—go away!" she exclaimed.

Furious, Toninho grabbed a candle from one of the offerings and hurled it into the waves, shouting,

"You can go to hell, Yemanjá!"

A hush fell over the crowd. What Toninho had done was nothing short of a sacrilege. Yemanjá was not going to take this lightly...

When Isabella arrived in San Francisco, to her great dismay, Monica wasn't there. Isabella had never been alone before and didn't know how she would survive without her best friend's support. They had helped each other through difficult times since they were children. When other kids made fun of them—the boy in the dress and the little puking girl—they always stuck together. And now, more then ever, Isabella needed the strength, guidance, and even the zest for life only Monica could provide.

Lonely and tormented, Isabella found her first week in San Francisco devastating. Even with her extraordinary culinary skills, becoming a chef in a strange, new city seemed impossible. She wandered the streets endlessly, facing rejection after rejection, and cried her broken heart to sleep every night.

The only job she was able to get was a mere teaching position at the Culinary Academy—a course for beginners. Even then, her yearning for Toninho was so intense that she would start sobbing uncontrollably in the middle of class.

Yemanjá had given her the strength to leave Toninho, and Isabella hoped that distance and time would ease the unbearable pain of being without him. But the ache only grew worse. In spite of his betrayal, she still loved him. It was all so maddening and confusing! She couldn't forgive him, but she couldn't live without him, and she felt haunted by his absence.

His scent seemed to follow her *everywhere.*

Even her wedding band, which she desperately tried to remove, seemed glued to her finger.

Below the equator, a similar agony had overtaken her husband. Since he had cursed Yemanjá, Toninho found his fortunes reversing. The fish had stopped coming to Bahia, and Isabella wasn't there to improvise in the kitchen. His restaurant was losing customers. But what troubled him most was how much he missed his wife. He couldn't eat, drink, or sleep without her. He couldn't even enter the kitchen, because even the aroma of chili peppers would torture him with memories of Isabella.

Plagued by the suspicion that his wife had fled to Monica's home in San Francisco, Toninho impulsively hopped on a plane one night with the Troubadours, the three musicians from his restaurant, intending to serenade Isabella back into his life.

When Monica finally returned from her adventures, she found Isabella deep in despair. Learning about Toninho's infidelity, Monica became philosophical. She knew a thing or two about being a man. She was born one, after all. "Men are not like us: faithful, nurturing, selective. Believe me, I know. And yet," she continued with a sigh, "we love the naughty devils anyway."

"What I have with Toninho is not love. It's a curse!" Isabella cried to her friend. "If I want to start a new life, I have to take him out of my head, out of my heart, out of me!"

Monica knew there was only one solution for Isabella: Serafina, the witch doctor.

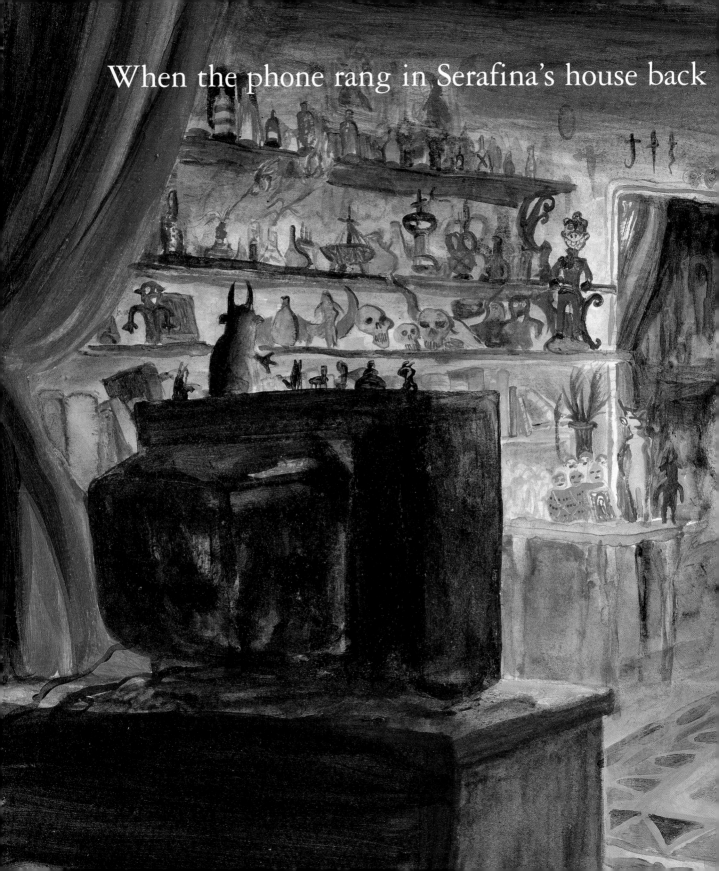

When the phone rang in Serafina's house back

in Bahia, she already knew of Isabella's plight.

This was an unusual request that would need an unusual solution. Serafina consulted the cowry shells, which fell from her cupped hands and scattered haphazardly on the floor. After studying each shell and the piles into which they fell, she spoke in a warning tone, "I can help you, child, but the spell is irreversible. Yemanjá will take your love to the bottom of the sea and you will never love Toninho again. So you must be certain that this is what you really want. Are you sure you are prepared for that?"

Monica looked at her friend anxiously, wondering what she would say. Isabella gulped down a breath, then without hesitation, replied, "Yes." She meticulously wrote down Serafina's love-revoking recipe.

Recipe for Removing Love

1 Coconut Flan (see separate recipe)
4 eyes of two boiled catfish
4 Mephisthophelean crabs
2 ripe female mangoes
1 heart of artichoke
1 necklace of black raisins
12 drops of midnight rain
1 feather of a black rooster
The beloved's photograph

Place the coconut flan in the center of a blue platter and lay the four catfish eyes around it in the four cardinal points: north, south, east, west. Set the four crabs exactly between the catfish eyes. Cut the ripe female mangoes in eight strips and arrange them around the flan. Mash the artichoke heart and spoon it over the mangoes. Surround the flan with the necklace of black raisins and shower it with midnight rain. Insert the rooster feather on top of the flan and, finally, sprinkle the ashes of your beloved's photograph over the entire dish.

Take the offering to the beach during a full moon. Enter the shallows and count each wave that comes to you, chanting "odoiá." Place the offering on the seventh wave and let it drift. Close your eyes and say a silent prayer to Yemanjá, declaring your intent, then walk away without looking back.

Coconut Flan

- 4 tablespoons cornstarch
- 2 cups cold whole milk
- 1½ cups thick coconut milk
- ¾ cup sugar

Dissolve the cornstarch in half a cup of the milk. In a bowl, combine the rest of the milk, coconut milk, sugar, and dissolved cornstarch. Transfer it to a heavy, nonreactive saucepan over medium heat, whisking the mixture constantly for about 10 minutes or until it comes to a boil. Lower the heat and continue whisking for 3 more minutes. Remove from the stove, pour into a well-buttered mold, and refrigerate overnight.

To serve, unmold the flan onto a platter. If you're not using it for the purposes of a spell, the Coconut Flan makes a scrumptious dessert that can be served with figs, peaches, or Prunes in Heavy Syrup:

Prunes in Heavy Syrup

- 2 cups pitted prunes
- 1 cup sugar
- 2 cinnamon sticks
- 3 cups water

In a saucepan, combine the prunes, sugar, cinnamon sticks, and water. Bring to a boil, lower heat to medium, and cook, covered, for about 1 hour. Serve over the Coconut Flan.

That very night, after preparing the offering, Isabella carried it under the full moon to the sea. A dense, almost otherworldly fog surrounded her. Her face glowed from the light of the candle adorning the tray. Isabella stepped into the ocean, and as each wave caressed her feet, she chanted "odoiá." After the seventh wave, she laid the tray on the water and pushed it out to sea. The offering drifted, surely, as if it had a destiny. As it made its way farther out, the water around it became agitated, forming a whirlpool that engulfed the offering.

Overwhelmed by Yemanjá's response,
Isabella closed her eyes, swooning, as if
caught in the whirlpool herself.

As she silently declared her intent, she could almost see the deep, dark world of caves and tentacles and fluorescent jellyfish. The air was charged with electricity. A bolt of lightning flared across the sky, followed by a boom of thunder! Amidst the phantasmagoric creatures, the silvery scales of the mermaid goddess flashed by, her tail whipping through the water, her wavy hair swirling around her as she waited for the offering.

At that very moment, Toninho was flying across the continent to San Francisco, listening to the hopeful music of the Troubadours. Despite the troubles, he was convinced he would bring back his wife. Suddenly, lightning struck the plane, causing it to jolt! Toninho's eyes widened with fear.

Under the sea, the offering slowly descended while the candle magically kept burning brightly. On the shore, following strict instructions, Isabella walked away without looking back.

Isabella woke up with a new sensation in her body. She felt light, free, full of joy. Everything around her also seemed different: the morning light more golden, the colors more intense, the sounds of the city like music. Even the wedding band she had so desperately tried to remove no longer made her sad. In fact, it slid right off her finger as if by magic. Isabella jumped off the bed and happily danced her way to the kitchen to make her special blend of morning coffee:

Coffee with Clove and Cinnamon

2 cups water

4 tablespoons espresso,
   ground extra fine

Brown sugar to taste

1 cinnamon stick

1 whole clove

Place the water in a small pan over medium heat. When it's almost boiling, add the coffee, brown sugar, cinnamon, and clove. Remove from the stove before the water rises and pour the thick infusion into a filter.

As the coffee flowed from the filter into Isabella's cup, a light vapor rose and traveled out the window like a thin veil. Its tendrils made their way around the street, rousing all the neighbors. It even crept through the window of an ambitious television producer named Cliff, who found himself enraptured by its intoxicating aroma.

Charmed like a serpent, Cliff followed his nose out of his apartment and into the street, where he was stunned to find the most enchanting woman he had ever seen. In a breezy, flower-print dress, Isabella walked down the street, her long cinnamon hair blowing in the wind, her graceful body swinging like a samba. Her sensuality was completely unself-conscious, yet it was powerful enough to disrupt the entire city. Everywhere she passed, heads turned, traffic stopped, women held on to their husbands! Construction workers dropped their tools and went after Isabella. A policeman made a U-turn. A fragile old man threw away his cane.

In a matter of minutes, Isabella walked like the Pied

Piper of San Francisco, a trail of men at her heels.

At the Culinary Academy, Isabella swayed past the student chefs, and trays of dishes and boxes of supplies came crashing down in her wake. She reached the classroom and flashed a radiant smile at the group of students, who now included Cliff, the construction workers, the policeman, the old man without a cane, the wives holding on to their husbands, and the sea of men from the street. Happy to see so many people interested in cooking, she started her class. "Good morning. I'm Isabella Oliveira. Welcome to *Passion Food*! Today, we're going to make my favorite dish from Bahia: Coconut Shrimp, *Moqueca de Camarão*." The students took down the recipe:

Moqueca de Camarão

(Coconut Shrimp)

2 pounds fresh, medium to large shrimp

Juice of 4 limes

Olive oil

2 medium onions, 1½ minced, ½ sliced

3 cloves garlic, minced

4 tomatoes, 3 diced, 1 sliced

2 red bell peppers, 1½ diced, ½ sliced

1 small chili pepper (preferably malagueta), minced

1 bouquet of cilantro, washed and minced

Salt to taste

4 cups Coconut Milk (fresh is better—see separate recipe)

Dende oil (Brazilian palm oil, famous for its golden color,
  found only in specialty stores; optional)

(You may want to save the shrimp shells to make stock. Simply cover the shells with water, bring to a boil, and let simmer. Add a ladle of stock to the recipe if more sauce is desired. Also, use as much chili pepper as you like, depending on how spicy you want the dish. Remember to coat your fingers with oil when chopping the chili so your skin won't get burned.)

Devein and rinse the shrimp, then place them in the fresh lime juice to marinate.

Coat the bottom of a large skillet with olive oil and heat over medium to high heat. Sauté the minced onions, garlic, diced tomatoes, diced bell peppers, chili pepper, and cilantro until the onions are translucent. Salt to taste. Add the shrimp to the cooked vegetables and cover with the sliced onion, sliced tomato, and sliced bell pepper. Pour in the coconut milk, add a lace of dende oil, and cook until the shrimp turn pink and begin to curl. Add more salt if necessary.

Serve the luscious Coconut Shrimp over a bed of rice.

Coconut Milk

1 coconut

(When selecting coconuts, choose one that is heavy for its size. Shake well to make sure it is full of water. Avoid any coconut with damp "eyes." Unopened coconuts can be stored at room temperature for up to five months.)

Drain the coconut water by piercing two of the three "eyes" with an ice pick. Place the coconut water in a small saucepan and warm it over very low heat. Heat the coconut by placing it in a 350°F oven for 10 to 15 minutes. The coconut will develop fault lines. Take the coconut outside, place it on newspaper, and hit it along the fault lines with a hammer. The coconut should open after a couple of strikes. Remove the meat from the coconut shell and peel the brown skin with a paring knife. Grate the coconut, preferably using a hand grater. This is hard work, but it is worth every drop of sweat—like all good things in life. One coconut yields 3 to 4 cups grated meat.

Wrap the grated coconut in cheesecloth, making a tight pouch, and dip it into the warm (not hot) coconut water. The pouch will expand, absorbing the water like a sponge. Squeeze the pouch over a bowl, extracting as much of the milk as possible. This batch is referred to as "thick coconut milk."

In case this doesn't produce the necessary 4 cups of coconut milk, here's how to make more:

When all the coconut water has been absorbed from the pan, repeat this process using regular water that has been warming over a low flame. This batch is called "thin coconut milk."

Now you have plenty of coconut milk for cooking!

"Cooking is more fun when you're fully involved in the transformation of the food," said Isabella to her students, who, following her instructions, squeezed the pouches of grated coconut, feeling the creamy milk flow between their fingers. "To experience the alchemy taking place right at your fingertips, you must relax and enjoy the process. When you surrender to the sensations, magical things can happen…" Isabella was right. Preparing the food became an aphrodisiac. Imbued with a new kind of radiance, the students began to work together in couples, smiling and flirting with each other. Gradually, they forgot all rules of politeness, loosening their shirts, even embracing… Cooking together, they felt completely transformed!

When the students splashed coconut milk over the shrimp, the dish reached its full potential, infused with a smooth, silky richness. Isabella fearlessly shook the skillet, flipping the contents in a swooping wave of sauce. Beads of sweat ran down her neck, nourishing the white rosebud pinned to her dress. The bud, in turn, opened, revealing its innermost petals in the heat of her cleavage.

"Remember, it will taste even better if you share it with someone you love," she concluded. **Cliff saw Isabella through a veil of steam.** His heart yearned for her, but the ambitious producer in him was already picturing the sultry beauty cooking on her own television show.

"So what do you think?" asked Cliff, after the lesson. "A cooking show, just like the class. Your recipes, your style, everything just the way you want." Isabella beamed. This was a thousand times better than anything she had ever dreamed of!

A star was about to be born…

For the premiere of the show, Isabella wore a stunning scarlet-red Baiana dress, strings of blue beads around her neck, and a white rosebud in her décolletage. Her cinnamon curls cascaded in endless mounds over her shoulders, making her look more Brazilian than ever. Before the cameras started to roll, she closed her eyes and prayed nervously, "Yemanjá, I dedicate this dish to you. Please don't let me down…" Cliff chewed on a pencil, also nervous. But when the show went on the air, Isabella was suddenly filled with confidence. She lit up the screen with her smile and addressed the audience. "Good evening. I'm Isabella Oliveira. Welcome to *Passion Food*! On this show, you will learn to transform simple ingredients into sensual, lusty dishes that fire the blood and satisfy the heart." Cliff knew they were going to hit the jackpot. Then, to everyone's surprise, Isabella announced, **"Before we begin, I would like to introduce my assistant, Monica."** Batting her long lashes, Monica appeared in front of the cameras decked out in a Carmen Miranda costume. She was an immediate hit!

Meanwhile, the persistent Toninho and his band of Troubadours were combing San Francisco, searching for Isabella. At first, he was optimistic, and the Troubadours sang happy songs. "She's out there somewhere. I can feel it!" he declared, "and though she may be cooking in another restaurant, at least I know one thing. She would never even *look* at another man!"

But as the days went on, the Troubadours' songs became melancholic. Isabella seemed to have vanished from the face of the earth...

Toninho wandered the streets, dejected. Behind him, the Troubadours hovered like guardian angels, plucking the heartbreaking strings of their guitars. At the corner, three ladies of the night, leaning against lampposts, caught the musicians' attention and hearts. Seeing this, Toninho dismissed his faithful companions. "Take the night off. There's no Isabella to serenade anyway."

Alone, Toninho entered Henry's Tavern, oblivious to his surroundings, and sat at the bar. He longed for a *caipirinha,* a Brazilian cocktail—the perfect drink to drown his sorrows. Isabella always made it this way:

Classic Caipirinha

1 lime, washed and cut into quarters (without removing the skin)
2 tablespoons brown sugar
2 ounces of cachaça, a Brazilian spirit (may be replaced with vodka, which will give the drink a slightly different taste)
Crushed ice

Place the lime sections in a small, round-bottomed glass. Add the sugar and crush the lime with a pestle, until its juice mixes with the sugar. Add the cachaça, stir, and add the crushed ice.

Also, caipirinhas should always be made one at a time.

Passion Fruit Caipirinha

1 passion fruit
2 tablespoons brown sugar
2 ounces cachaça
Crushed ice

Cut the passion fruit in half, remove the pulp (including the seeds), and place it in a small, round-bottomed glass. Add the sugar and mash it into the passion fruit pulp with a pestle. Add cachaça, stir, and add the crushed ice.

Unfortunately, however, Toninho had to settle for whiskey. After knocking back the shot, he heard a familiar voice: "Soak a small loaf of stale bread in the coconut milk and work it with your fingers until it's pulpy and completely wet."

Toninho arched an eyebrow and looked at his drink. He had only had *one* shot… "Am I losing my mind?" But the familiar voice persisted. Finally, he turned his gaze to the television and had the shock of his life! There she was, *his* Isabella, cooking on the screen with an unsettling energy, her dress clinging to the sweat on her skin. "Isabella!"

The men in the bar stared at her like dazed puppets. Toninho charged toward the TV. "That's my wife!" he exclaimed. But the customers thought he was just drunk. "Oh yeah," one of them asked with a smirk, "do you work *her* until she's pulpy?" Toninho defended his wife's honor with a blow to the heckler's chin, sending him reeling backward, crashing onto a table! The dazed victim recovered and took a swing at Toninho, but Toninho ducked and another customer got hit instead. A brawl ensued . . .

Punches flew, glass shattered, bar stools broke.
on the floor, writhing in pain.

The fight raged on until all the men were lying

On TV, Isabella concluded the show with some final words and a devastating smile. "Simmer for a few minutes and serve hot over a bed of rice. Well-seasoned rice is a staple in Brazilian kitchens. No meal is complete without this simple, yet essential dish. And remember, it will taste even better if you share it with someone you love."

Isabella's Brazilian Rice

2 cups long-grain rice
Canola oil
1 medium onion, minced
2 cloves garlic, minced
Salt to taste
1½ cups water
½ cup coconut milk

Rinse the rice in cold water at least twice.

Cover the bottom of a saucepan with canola oil. Heat the oil over a medium to high heat and sauté the onion and garlic until translucent. Add the rice, stirring constantly, for about 1 minute. Make sure the rice is well coated with oil, onion, and garlic. Add salt to taste. Bring the water to a boil and add it to the rice mixture. Add the coconut milk and stir so it doesn't stick together. Bring the new mixture to a boil, then lower the heat, cover the pan, and simmer for about 20 minutes, or until the rice has absorbed all the water.

In Brazil, rice accompanies a variety of dishes but, most commonly, black beans. Like Romeo and Juliet, rice and beans are never too far apart…

Black Beans

4 cups dry black beans

8 cups cold water

1 or 2 bay leaves

Olive oil

1 medium onion, minced

3 cloves garlic, minced

Salt and pepper to taste

Pinch of cumin

Bacon (optional)

Carefully sort the beans to remove any stones, rinse them well, and soak them overnight.

The next day, discard the water and put the plumped beans into a large pot, adding 8 cups cold water and the bay leaves. Cover the pot and bring to a boil. Lower the heat and let simmer for about 1½ hours, or until the beans are tender.

(Beans should always start cooking in cold water. If more water must be added after the beans are cooking, that water should be boiling. Also, cooked beans freeze very well. If you plan to freeze a portion of the beans, do so at this point, before seasoning. When you are ready to defrost the beans, season them according to the following instructions.)

Cover the bottom of a small saucepan with olive oil and heat over medium heat. Sauté the onion and garlic until translucent. Add a generous amount of salt and pepper, a pinch of cumin, and bacon, if desired. Put one full ladle of cooked beans into saucepan to absorb all the seasonings that have been brewing. Pour this mixture into the rest of the cooked beans, mixing well. Add more salt if necessary. Let the newly seasoned beans boil uncovered for 15 minutes.

Serve the glistening black beans over a bed of rice and, if you have access to these ingredients, sprinkle with Farofa.

Farofa

- 1 cup yucca meal
- 2 tablespoons dende oil (or substitute butter)

Place ingredients in a hot cast-iron skillet, lower the heat, and cook for a couple of minutes, stirring occasionally until the yucca meal has turned golden.

Serve sprinkled over rice and beans, with a side order of Kale.

Kale

3 bouquets fresh, large-leaf kale

Olive oil

1 small onion, minced

2 cloves garlic, minced

Salt and pepper to taste

Remove the center stalk of the leaves and rinse them well. Stack the leaves of each bunch on top of each other and roll them in a tube. Slice them into extra-thin, spaghetti-like strips.

Cover the bottom of a wide saucepan with olive oil and heat over medium heat. Sauté the onion and garlic with salt and pepper to taste. Add the kale strips, sautéing for about 2 minutes while stirring constantly. Add a few drops of water, cover the pan, and simmer over low heat for 10 minutes, or until wilted. Serve hot with rice and beans.

Isabella's magnetism and the exotic dishes she created made the show an immediate success! Not only did she teach her recipes in the most enticing way, but she opened the minds of viewers to a whole new cuisine. *Passion Food* was the talk of the town.

Toninho was waiting outside the television station when Isabella exited the main door, beaming like a newborn star. She froze in shock when she saw him pushing his way through the crowd toward her. But under the neon light, she noticed the bruises on his face, and forgetting her surprise, she reached out her hand with concern.

"Toninho . . . what happened to your face?"

"What happened to my face?" he replied scoldingly. "I was defending your honor, that's what happened to my face!"

Isabella's tone became icy. "My honor does not need defending."

His anger grew. "Oh, no? I traveled half the planet to find the Isabella I know and love, and I found you on TV, looking, looking…"

In that moment, as if the gods were conspiring, a truck with high beams passed behind Isabella, lighting her hair from behind with the most incredible glow. Her beauty was so striking, time seemed to stand still. Toninho was at a loss…

"You look so beautiful . . . like when we first met and I made you my wife. Your skin tasted of salt, your hair held the scent of cinnamon, and when you kissed me, your lips burned with chili peppers. It made my head spin. . . . Please, Isabella, come home with me where you belong."

His words were full of passion and longing, but Isabella didn't feel a thing. "I belong where I choose to be and I choose to be here," she replied.

Toninho snapped out of his trance and looked at his wife with a more critical eye. "Do you also choose to dress like this? It's not proper. Not in your condition."

"What condition?"

"Married. To me."

Indignant, Isabella replied, "Funny, you don't act married."

"No? Three years I've been lying flat on my back for you. Three years! Not to mention little things like I never get to drive anywhere. You can't just move me around like a puppet!"

"Fine. From now on you can move however you like. Good-bye, Toninho," Isabella said as she turned to leave.

Trying to stop her, Toninho grabbed her by the hand. He realized she was no longer wearing her wedding band, but before he could protest, his wife pulled herself free and breezed away.

Isabella refused to see him again. Not only did she ignore his phone calls but she returned the dozens of shimmering white roses he sent. Baffled by her behavior and quickly running out of options, Toninho knew he had to think of another plan…

That evening, with his band of Troubadours, Toninho snuck into the television studio. The security guards were so mesmerized watching Isabella on the monitors they didn't notice the four intruders. Isabella was on the air, preparing a delicious banana dessert.

"Trust your senses," she said, beaming. "Don't just rely on a timer. Learn to use your eyes and nose. Also, don't be afraid to use your fingers to measure ingredients. In time, you'll develop a tactile memory for just the right amount, and the knowledge of how to prepare a dish will live forever in your hands."

This was the dessert Isabella was preparing when she had the surprise of her life:

Fried Bananas

Butter
Ripe bananas, cut lengthwise
Brown sugar to taste
Cinnamon powder to taste
Pinch of clove powder
Boiling water, or a sweet after-dinner liqueur such as Grand Marnier
Vanilla ice cream

Let your senses tell you how much of each ingredient you need. Melt a generous amount of butter in a large, hot skillet and sauté the banana slices. Add lots of brown sugar, cinnamon powder, and a pinch of clove powder. The sugar and spices will melt into the butter, forming a caramel-like sauce. When the banana slices become soft and bronzed by the spices, add a splash of boiling water or sweet liqueur to the sauce. Serve hot over vanilla ice cream.

In the middle of Isabella's presentation, Toninho stepped right in front of the cameras and began to sing.

When she heard his voice, Isabella was rendered speechless. Monica took a swig of the Grand Marnier. The entire crew stared at him, aghast! But the show was live and had to go on. Isabella swallowed her rage and resumed her cooking, trying to ignore his presence. But his song was so beautiful, its rhythm so contagious, that little by little everybody found themselves bewitched.

Nos braços de Isabel eu sou mais homen
Nos braços de Isabel eu sou um deus
Os braços de Isabel são meu conforto
Quando deixo o quais do porto
Pra viver os sonhos meus…

In the arms of Isabel I am a man

In the arms of Isabel I am a god

The arms of Isabel are my comfort

When I leave the harbor

To pursue my dreams…

The cameras started to sway to his tempo, and the gaffer dimmed the lights to follow the enchanting melody. Even the caramel sauce Isabella was preparing bubbled to his infectious beat. It was amazing how synchronized they were! There was no denying that Toninho's sensual rhythm perfectly matched her movements. Watching incredulously from backstage, the producers realized they had a gold mine on their hands. Isabella closed the show as Toninho was ending his song… "and remember, it will taste even better when you share it with someone you love."

As soon as the cameras stopped rolling, she grabbed a bunch of bananas and clobbered Toninho. "Are you out of your mind?" But in spite of Isabella's protests, Toninho was hired immediately. He smiled at his wife, feeling smug and triumphant. Isabella knew of only two ways to get rid of her husband: quit the show or give him the opportunity to hang himself. The second choice seemed like a much better option…

The next day, *Passion Food* was recorded live in an open-air market. Dozens of stands were filled with luxurious tropical fruits, trellises were laden with all kinds of exotic vegetables, and a crowd of extras and fans stood by. Isabella's cooking table was decorated with extraordinary sculptures made from melons, mangoes, and papayas. Shimmying to Toninho's music, she carved a pineapple into an exotic flower. Her fans roared with enthusiasm when she held up the finished masterpiece.

During a commercial break, Toninho approached Isabella and whispered in her ear, "Give me a kiss." This was the moment she was waiting for… Isabella smiled but shook her head. Then, looking straight into his eyes, she dropped the bomb: "I think we should get a divorce."

Toninho stared at her in utter disbelief while she walked back to her table and prepared to go on the air. As the cameras began to roll, he exploded, "I'll never give you a divorce! You're my wife and I love you!" The whole crew became paralyzed. Then Cliff started shouting, the director cried, and the fans gasped! Oblivious to the chaos he was causing, Toninho raged on and on. But to Isabella's great dismay, Toninho was not fired. His uncontrollable passion had once more turned disaster to his advantage.

The ratings shot up! People called in, demanding to see more real-life romance in the cooking show.

Recovering from the fight in Monica's trailer, Toninho complained, "I can't believe she is punishing me so hard for one little mistake."

Monica tried to make him understand that his *little* mistake was not so little and was just the tip of the iceberg. He had stifled Isabella from the beginning, stashing her away in the kitchen.

"Start with the basics," Monica advised. "Try to be her friend. Look at Cliff. He knows how to be her friend and she seems to like him."

"Cliff?" Toninho replied. "What could she possibly see in that clown?"

Monica held back a mischievous smile, "Apart from the fact that he is sweet, modern, and sensitive, don't you think he's sexy?"

Toninho was consumed by jealousy, but he had to admit that Cliff must have been doing something right. For the first time, Toninho was struck by the realization that maybe he wasn't as perfect as he thought…

Following Monica's advice, Toninho patiently waited outside Isabella's building. When she appeared, he *humbly* asked her to give him another chance.

"No," Isabella said firmly.

Desperate, Toninho pleaded, "For each person there is only one perfect mate. The moment we met, I knew it was you and you knew it was me. If we give up now, we will never love this way again."

"Who gave up, me or you?" she asked solemnly.

Her words cut him like a knife. "I didn't give up. I made a mistake. Please, Isabella, don't leave me. I'll do anything you want," he cried.

Her answer was definitive. "Don't make it harder, Toninho. I can be your friend, but I just don't love you anymore. I'm sorry." She walked away.

Toninho knew then that he was losing her forever. Forlorn, he began to realize his mistakes. Not only had he stifled his wife, but he had betrayed her because of a mere *position*. How could he have been so foolish? Now all seemed lost, and the pain of living without her was excruciating. His sadness became so overwhelming that clouds covered the sky and the days became long and dark. Even when he sang on Isabella's show, Toninho's voice was filled with *saudades,* a profound and painful longing. And when he closed his eyes, he could almost taste her kisses . . . her lips burning into his with the fire of malagueta peppers . . . the spicy peppers she used to make her favorite hot sauce.

Malagueta Sauce

3 to 4 malagueta peppers, minced (or substitute another extra-spicy pepper)

1 to 2 cloves garlic

Salt to taste

1 medium onion, minced

2 tablespoons fresh cilantro, minced (if desired)

Juice of 4 limes

Crush the malagueta peppers, garlic, and salt in a mortar until they form a paste. Mix the onion, cilantro, and lime juice into the paste. Cover with plastic wrap and let it sit at room temperature for about 1 hour.

(Before handling a chili pepper, remember to coat your fingers with oil so your skin won't get burned.)

Serve over rice and beans, or any other dish that could use a little heat!

Toninho's anguish started to affect everyone in the show. Even Isabella began to feel an inexplicable tinge of melancholy, even though the show was more popular than ever. The emptiness she was feeling was beginning to bother her, and she confessed to Monica. "Everything is going so well, but I feel as if the wind were blowing right through me."

Monica had the perfect solution for her friend. "You have to fall in love again —and fast."

"I'm not in the mood for love." Isabella sighed.

"It takes an effort, girl," Monica insisted. "If you don't eat, you don't get hungry."

To Monica, Cliff seemed to be the perfect dish for that occasion.

That evening, Isabella went out to dinner with Cliff. She knew that he was falling for her, but no matter how hard she tried, she just didn't share his feelings. In fact, she was beginning to think she couldn't feel anything anymore. There was a numbness inside her. For the first time, Isabella began to question the choice she had made. Drowning her feelings had been the quick and easy way out of the pain. But had it been the best solution?

To make things worse, the show was going national and a group of powerful network executives arrived to take charge. They immediately began eliminating certain details they thought were too exotic: dress style, cooking ingredients, personnel. They didn't realize that the strength of the show had been Isabella's authentic approach to Brazilian cuisine and traditions. Even Cliff, who had once promised Isabella the world, couldn't, or wouldn't, help her in the end.

Furious, she confronted him. "How can you go along with this?"

But Cliff was torn by his own ambition. "Isabella, you're a star now. This is bigger than you. It's not your decision anymore."

The malagueta sauce was switched to Tabasco sauce, her baiana-style dresses replaced by something less ethnic, and her resourceful assistant, Monica, dismissed. To calm herself, Isabella held a pearly conch shell to her ear and listened to the ebb and flow of the ocean. Her mind whirled inside the spiraling tunnels of the shell until it reached the shore…

On the beach, Toninho approached the water, holding a string of pearls in his hands. He looked drawn, tired, unshaven. The mischievous gleam in his eyes had disappeared. He cried to the sea, calling the goddess. "Yemanjá! I offer you these pearls so you'll forgive me for cursing you. But about Isabella, stay out of my business. This is her decision, and mine. When human love is strong enough, no god, not even you, can take it away." And hurling the pearls into the sea, he concluded, "Yemanjá be praised."

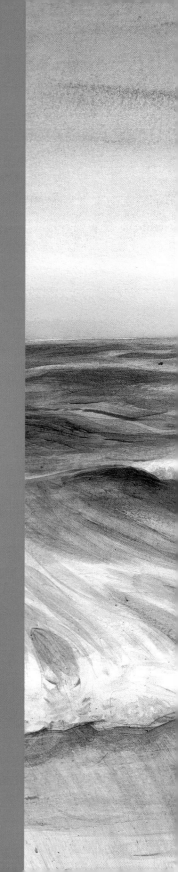

Back in the studio, Isabella set down the conch shell and the sound of the waves dissipated. She knew she had to quit the show.

That night, the passionate sounds of strings entered Monica's apartment, breaking the slumbering silence. Monica woke and approached the window. Her eyes widened when she saw Toninho and an orchestra of street musicians silhouetted against the radiant moon. They performed the most romantic serenade anyone had ever heard. Women appeared on their balconies to listen. Passersby stopped in their tracks.

"Isabella, come see this," Monica urged her friend. Isabella got up and peeked out the window. The melody pierced the darkness like a shooting star. It escalated and rhapsodized around Isabella until her spirit was pulled heavenward...

Isabella's feeling of emptiness was replaced by a profound longing—though for what, she no longer knew...

Auge da saudade me maltrata
Desta ingrata que não me sai do pensamento
Cresce o meu tormento
Trégoas a minha dor
Ressaibos do meu triste amor...

Oh, how this longing pains me
Your image is embedded in my thoughts
My torment grows
My pain has no relief
From the memory of our love...

Toninho stopped singing, and his plea rose above the orchestra. "Isabella! I want you to lead when we dance! I want you to drive the car! I want you on top! I wouldn't want you any other way!" As the music crescendoed, Isabella moved to the balcony, where she locked eyes with Toninho. His gaze was sincere and full of love. Isabella plucked the rose from her robe and tossed it to him.

The reckless rose glided its way into Toninho's waiting hand, streaking the night with its brilliant, incandescent white.

Toninho triumphantly caught the rose in midair as the music exploded in a deliverance of pure joy. He climbed the fire escape to Isabella's balcony and approached his beloved.

Isabella could see how much he had changed. "Why couldn't you have been like this before?" she said. "Now it's too late."

"Kiss me, then tell me that," Toninho replied.

A spark of hope flickered in her eyes. Toninho held her in his arms and kissed her with alarming hunger. At that moment, a warning flash of lightning ripped across the sky!

Water seemed to ripple over the lovers as they kissed. On the ocean floor, Isabella's offering was guarded by an army of sea creatures. The candle was still burning brightly…

The kiss ended, and Toninho pulled himself away from Isabella. She opened her eyes, full of dread. She couldn't feel anything! Even worse, she could see the flame of the candle reflected in Toninho's pupils—the candle from her offering, binding her to the wish she had made. Isabella stepped back in horror. Toninho's eyes swelled, but even his tears couldn't extinguish the flame burning in his pupils. With a huge knot in his throat, he climbed down the balcony and walked away, accompanied by his faithful minstrels. Despondent, Isabella watched him go. "What have I done…!"

That very night, Isabella frantically began to prepare an offering for Yemanjá. Monica reminded her that the spell was irreversible, but Isabella didn't want to hear it. She furiously beat the eggs for a mouthwatering Brazilian soufflé, following an old family recipe that she hoped would break the spell.

Hearts of Palm Soufflé

One small onion, minced
1 clove garlic, crushed
2 tablespoons butter
2 tomatoes, skinned and diced
1 can hearts of palm, diced
Salt and pepper to taste
½ cup flour
2 cups milk
4 eggs, separated
½ cup grated Parmesan cheese
Bread crumbs

Preheat the oven to 375°F.

Sauté the onion and garlic in 1 tablespoon melted butter over medium heat. Add the tomatoes and hearts of palm. Season with salt and pepper to taste and set aside.

Melt the rest of the butter in a separate pan. Mix the flour into the butter, then add the milk, stirring constantly until it thickens. Remove from the heat. Stir in the egg yolks, the hearts of palm mixture, and the Parmesan cheese.

In a separate bowl, beat the egg whites until stiff. Fold the egg whites into the soufflé mixture.

Grease a round baking dish with butter and sprinkle the bottom and sides with bread crumbs. Spoon the soufflé mixture into the dish and bake until it turns slightly golden.

Serve immediately.

Isabella removed the soufflé from the oven. It looked magnificent, its puffy golden head rising out of the dish and swaying ever so gently as she transported it to the counter. Then, a startling thing happened. The soufflé collapsed, deflating right before her eyes! Isabella felt like a magician who had just lost her powers. She sensed Yemanjá was punishing her for going back on her word.

Panicked, she cried to her friend. "Look! Everything is ruined! I can't cook anymore…!"

Always pragmatic, Monica looked quickly around the kitchen in search of a solution. She spotted a box of instant macaroni and cheese and grabbed it from the shelf.

"Use the soufflé as a base and pretty it up with this. Yemanjá will never know the difference."

What a sacrilege! Yemanjá was a great gourmet, with an incredibly refined palate. Isabella knew this, but what else could she do? Maybe if she included Yemanjá's favorite trinkets, small objects that appealed to her vanity, the goddess wouldn't pay attention to the food. Isabella placed a small mirror, a comb, a bottle of perfume, and a bouquet of white roses around the unappetizing dish.

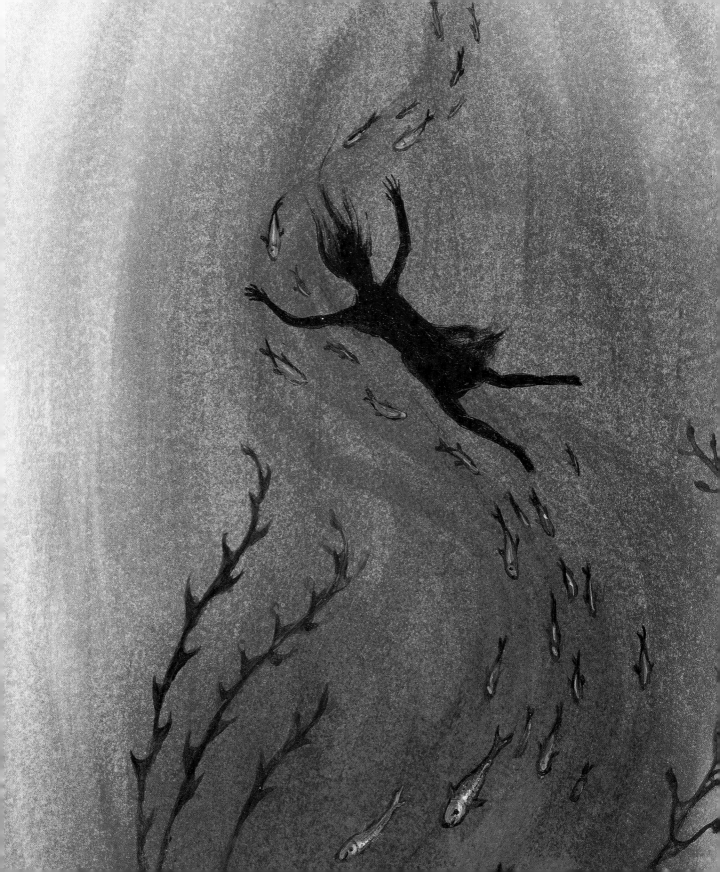

That night Isabella took the strange, new offering to the beach. The wind howled so loudly it almost upstaged the booming thunderclaps. Isabella stepped into the sea and braved the menacing waves, holding the tray above the foam and spray. She begged the powerful goddess, "Yemanjá, please don't reject my offering! Give me back my love!"

Thunder rolled and the wind whipped her hair, yet Isabella persevered. But she was no match for the wrath of the sea. A gargantuan wave rose from the depths, and with a gasp, Isabella disappeared beneath it!

The young woman struggled against the wave with all her might, but an unseen force was pulling her down. Exhausted and realizing there was nothing she could do to stop her descent, Isabella surrendered, and her lithe figure floated gracefully to the bottom of the sea.

Strangely, the silence of this dark and mysterious world was almost comforting. Then, amid clusters of dancing seaweed, Yemanjá flashed before her eyes! Her scales changed colors as she whipped past Isabella, vanishing in a burst of bubbles. When the bubbles disappeared, Isabella could see her first offering on the ocean floor, the candle still glowing. The black rooster feather seemed to be waving at Isabella, inviting her to come closer. With renewed purpose, she swam toward the offering, determined to take it back. But when she reached out to grab it, there was a huge explosion of light!

When Isabella came to, she found herself cast in a heap on the shore. The mirror, the comb, the bouquet of roses—all the objects were being tossed around carelessly by the waves. Yemanjá had rejected the offering and refused to break the spell...

Dejected and resigned to her fate, Isabella went to the studio to pack her belongings. She had drowned her love, quit her job, lost her dreams. Isabella approached the dressing room mirror, which was covered with photographs and other souvenirs, and slowly started removing each item, closing this chapter of her life. "What am I going to do? I have nothing left."

At that moment, she heard a voice, "You still have me."

Isabella turned around to find Toninho emerging from the shadows, determined as if he had a mission. Surprised, she uttered, "Toninho . . . how did you know I was here?"

"Monica told me. She told me everything."

Isabella sighed, feeling defeated. "I wish there were something I could do. . ."

"There is," said Toninho, ready to challenge Yemanjá. "Why don't we cook something together and see what happens?"

Isabella was choked with emotion. "I'd love to, but I don't think I can cook anymore."

"Maybe together we can find an answer," he said hopefully.

The cooking set was bathed in a dim, almost sacred light. Isabella and Toninho approached the table—the altar upon which food and love came together in a sensual communion. Isabella nervously looked at the ingredients. She was eager to try, but scared she would fail. Toninho poured the

coconut milk over the yucca meal and guided Isabella's hands as they began to mix it, preparing a stuffing. The ingredients started to bind. "It's working!" Isabella exclaimed with gleaming eyes. Next, they filled a beautiful snapper with the mixture.

Reaching over Isabella, Toninho placed the snapper on the banana leaf. As they wrapped the fish in the leaf, their hands inadvertently touched. Toninho looked at Isabella, searching her eyes for some kind of sign. They continued working together in silence, commingling as if they were one. This was the recipe they followed:

Snapper in Banana Leaf

For the fish:
1 whole snapper, deboned
Salt and pepper to taste
2 cloves garlic, crushed
Juice of 1 lime

For the stuffing:
½ stick butter
1 small onion, minced
1 carrot, cut into thin slices
2 tomatoes, skinned and diced
½ cup cilantro, minced
Salt to taste
1 cup yucca meal (toasted)
2 cups coconut milk

1 large banana leaf
Olive oil

Preheat the oven to 400°F.

Rub the snapper with the salt, pepper, crushed garlic, and lime juice while your lover melts the butter and sautés the onion, carrot, tomatoes, and cilantro, seasoning with salt.

In a bowl, dig your fingers into the yucca meal while your lover pours the coconut milk over the mixture. Both of you should massage the meal and coconut milk until it amalgamates into a creamy substance.

Fold the yucca meal/coconut milk mixture into the vegetables in the pan for a few minutes, then remove from the heat while your lover places the banana leaf in the oven for one minute.

Stuff the snapper with the above mixture.

Grease the slightly wilted banana leaf with olive oil. With your lover's help, wrap the stuffed snapper in the banana leaf and place it in an uncovered baking dish.

Cook in the oven for 1 hour.

Serve hot, in a romantic setting.

When the dish had finished cooking, Toninho removed it from the oven and presented it proudly to Isabella. He cut the banana-leaf casing, and a tendril of aromatic vapor was released. Isabella and Toninho took in the entrancing aroma, knowing they had succeeded in preparing an exquisite dish. The vapor playfully coiled around the lovers, then, as if it were alive, it crept out the window, hovering over the streets and expanding into a thick, rolling fog.

Drifting like a magic carpet, the fog reached the bay and unfolded its essence upon the water. The water, in turn, became agitated, as if charged by a strange force. The vapor penetrated the sea, making its way down the shadowy, liquid world. Her wavy hair crawling with starfish and crabs, the goddess was sleeping peacefully on the ocean floor, unaware of the entrancing aroma that was about to envelop her . . .

Back at the studio, Toninho offered Isabella a forkful of the succulent fish. Savoring it, she closed her eyes, wanting to remember the moment forever. Suddenly, a roaring thunder shook the television studio!

Underwater, schools of fish swirled in a frenzy! Enraptured by the intoxicating fragrance of the lovers' creation, Yemanjá was overpowered by their passion, but enraged by their defiance! She swam in a spiraling fury, her hair and tail whipping the waters into a monstrous whirlpool.

Lightning ripped across the sky, filtering through the fog with an unreal brightness. Everyone stepped outside to witness the spectacular electrical storm! Cliff found himself on his balcony, gazing at Monica on her balcony across the street. A strange current of energy passed through his body and suddenly he felt himself falling in love with her . . . Monica returned his gaze, overwhelmed by feelings of her own.

Inside the television studio, a series of thunderclaps triggered an incredible power surge. Isabella and Toninho held on to each other, astounded, as the lights went berserk and sparks flew from the cable connections.

On the ocean floor, the offering quivered as Yemanjá poised to decide the fate of the lovers.

Suddenly, from the whirlpool's vortex, an explosion of pure force catapulted the offering skyward in a waterspout that shot miles high. A tremendous gale pushed the water from the spout over the bay where its salty mist enveloped the entire city.

A jolt of electricity shot up Isabella's spine, and everything around her seemed like a feverish, tumultuous blur! Then, without warning, the sprinkler system went off, showering the lovers.

"It's salty . . . it tastes like seawater!" Toninho exclaimed.

Isabella put a drop to her lips. It was seawater! Her expression began to change as every cell in her body was engulfed by a wave of feelings. Isabella's love for Toninho was alive again, its power almost frightening! Yemanjá had succumbed to the power of human love.

"Toninho . . . I love you!" said Isabella.

Those were the words Toninho wanted so much to hear. "You love me?"

"Yes!" she cried.

"Oh, Isabella . . ." he said with a sigh, "I love you . . ."

Toninho took her in his arms and they entered into a kiss as deep and stirring as the seven seas . . .

Back in Bahia, the ocean was once again abundant with life. The mermaid goddess splashed in and out of frothy waves, pleased with the lovers' triumph.

In their bedroom, Isabella descended upon Toninho like a tropical storm, making love—woman on top. Diamonds of sweat glistened on their skin as she rode him like a wave, the two lovers smiling with love and pleasure, together at last.

In their new restaurant, Isabella cooked in an open kitchen, surrounded by ecstatic patrons, while Toninho sang to the music of the Troubadours, happily watching his wife basking in the limelight.

Nearby, Monica and Cliff danced a spicy samba.

Outside the restaurant, an endless line of customers waited their turn to savor what they had heard were the most delectable dishes ever created. The line stretched across Bahia, Brazil, South America, around the world, and even the universe—if that were possible...

Thus ends the story of Isabella and her Toninho, two lovers who discovered that neither fame nor position nor divine intervention could extinguish the awesome and eternal power of true love.

"Maybe getting what you want isn't as rewarding as the journey to get there . . ."

The End